First Edition

ISBN-13: 978-1539937616
ISBN-10: 1539937615

For information about authoring or illustrating your own children's book, visit www.familyfables.org.

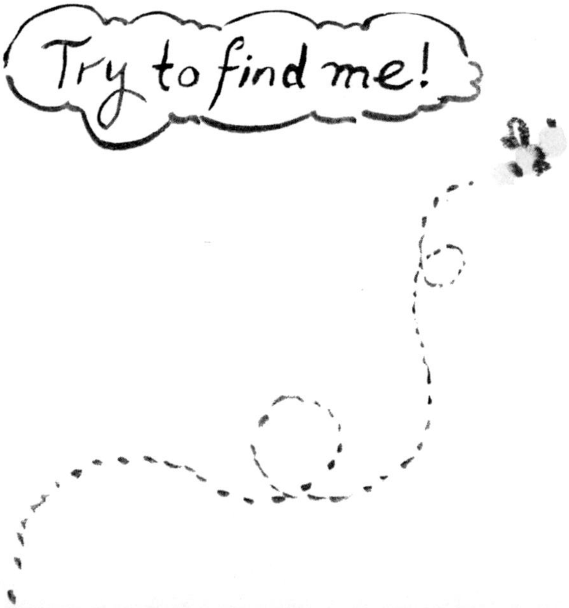
Try to find me!

Overjoyed to see the red fall leaves fall,
Gilroy belted out quite an odd turkey call.

Olivia the Owl was watching from above,
Then asked a question with her owly love.
"What was that my dear? That was no 'Hoo.'"

"That sounds so close," snapped the rooster on the roof,
"To what a bird should sound like, instead of that goof.
That thing on your face, we call it a beak.
Use it like mine, and speak bird speak."

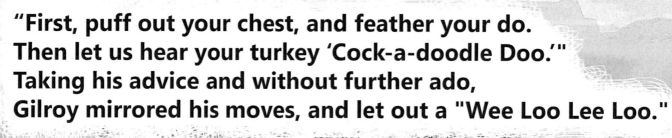

"First, puff out your chest, and feather your do.
Then let us hear your turkey 'Cock-a-doodle Doo.'"
Taking his advice and without further ado,
Gilroy mirrored his moves, and let out a "Wee Loo Lee Loo."

Interrupted by the pigeon perched on the fence,
"Hey, Gilroy the turkey! You look a little tense.
Don't mind the others. They haven't a clue.
The remedy you seek is in the form of a 'Coo.'"

"Jump up here with me, and follow my moves.
Then let us hear your turkey 'Coo Coo Ka Choo.'"
Taking his advice and without further ado,
Gilroy popped on the post and let out a "Wee Loo Lee Loo."

At the pond nearby swam a spotted looney loon.
"Come here young turkey, you've got to sing my tune."
Right then he yelled out, with not a moment to lose,
"Loo Loo Loo! Loo Dee Loo Dee Loo!"

Gilroy wandered off thinking, "I'm doing this all wrong. How am I going to find the right turkey song?"

Then off in the distance he heard a "Tut Tut To Do."
It came from a turkey but wasn't something he knew.

"You're not a loon, cow, rooster or owl.
You are who you are, Gilroy the fowl.
So no matter your call, make sure it's your own,
From the time you're a baby until you're full grown."

The advice sank in, as he looked all around.
Gilroy saw each animal sounding their sound.
They all looked happy, for they were who they were,
No matter what they wore: feathers or fur.

Gilroy smiled a big smile. He finally knew.
He was himself, a turkey through and through.
With that he joined the rest of the crew,
And let out his own Gilroy "Wee Loo Lee Loo!"

Made in the USA
San Bernardino, CA
24 October 2017